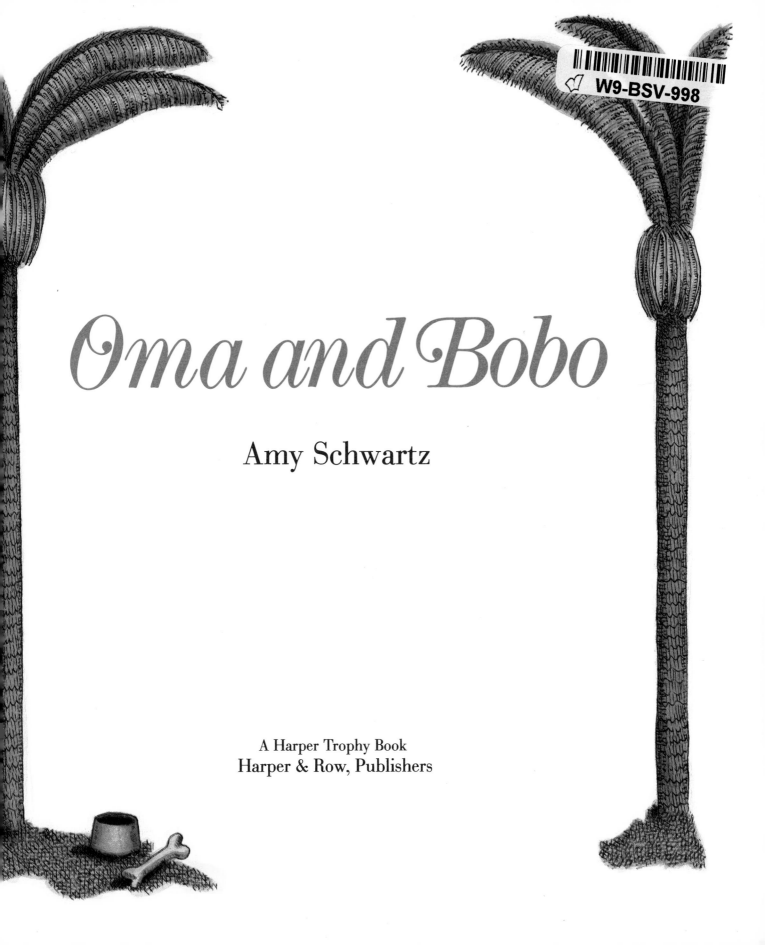

Oma and Bobo

Amy Schwartz

A Harper Trophy Book
Harper & Row, Publishers

For my grandmother
Lotte Herzberg
in memory

On Alice's birthday, her mother told her she could have a dog.
"Hurray! A puppy!" Alice cheered.
"*Mein Gott*," Oma said. "A dog."

Alice ran into the backyard to celebrate.
She practiced calling, "Fetch, King!" and "Attack, Brutus!"
until her mother came out with the car keys and said,
"We should get to the animal shelter before it closes."

At the shelter there were black dogs and brown dogs,
puppies and old dogs, beagles and terriers. But Alice could look only
at a black-and-white mutt napping in a soft ball in the corner.

"He's no longer a puppy," the attendant said.

"He doesn't look like a King or a Brutus," Alice's mother
remarked.

"But he's the one I want," said Alice.

When they got home, Alice showed the dog to her grandmother.
"What should I call him, Oma?"

"Trouble, Bother, and Nuisance. That's what I'd call him,"
Oma replied.

Alice petted her dog.

"Bobo," she said. "I'll call him Bobo."

She gave Bobo a slice of bologna from the refrigerator.

Oma locked herself in her room.

When Alice and Oma got up to cook breakfast, Bobo was chewing on Oma's old red potholder.

"*Du lieber Himmel!*" Oma cried. "What did I tell you? This dog must learn to behave himself, Alice. Just like every other person in this house.

"I am enrolling him in dog obedience school at once."

Alice and Bobo began lessons at Mr. Benjamin's School for Puppies that very afternoon.

Alice practiced with Bobo when they got home.
"Sit, Bobo!" Alice commanded.
Bobo looked up at the clouds.
"Fetch, Bobo!"
Bobo watched a robin fly by.
"A regular Rin Tin Tin," Oma said.
Alice gave Bobo a dog biscuit. "Don't worry, Bobo,"
she whispered. "You're a great dog. You'll do fine."

Bobo ate the biscuit. Then he trotted over to Oma.
He wagged his tail. Then he put his cold nose on her hand.

"*Dreckhund!*" Oma cried. She quickly wiped her hand on her apron
and went inside.

At the second lesson, Mr. Benjamin told the class about the dog show at the end of the term.

"Each dog who passes will get a blue ribbon," he said.

Mr. Benjamin smiled at a schnauzer, a doberman, and two poodle puppies.

Bobo was taking a nap.

"Some of our older participants," Mr. Benjamin observed, "might have a little trouble."

Alice scratched Bobo's favorite place on his belly.

Alice got up early the next morning to practice.

"Bobo's the smartest dog in his class," she said to Oma.
"Mr. Benjamin says that intelligence comes with age."

"That is true," Oma said. She watched Alice take Bobo
into the yard.

"Stay, Bobo!" Alice commanded.

Bobo stayed.

"Sit, Bobo!"

Bobo sat down.

"Good dog!" Alice said. She tossed a stick in the air.

"Fetch, Bobo!"

Bobo looked at the stick. Then he began digging a hole.

"Bobo!" Alice stamped her foot. "We'll never pass the dog show."

She sadly picked up her lunch box and turned to leave for school.

Bobo trotted inside.

"*Ach*, Bobo," Oma said. "At your age, such behavior? How do you expect to get Alice a blue ribbon?" She started washing the dishes.

"Are you eating right, Bobo? Not enough exercise, is that the problem?"

Bobo wagged his tail. Then he rolled over onto his back. He tapped Oma's foot with one paw.

Oma slowly lifted up her foot. And with the tip of her black shoe, she gently rubbed Bobo's favorite place on his belly.

When Alice got home from school, Oma and Bobo were not there. While Alice was eating her snack, Oma and Bobo came hurrying up the driveway.

"I just needed some exercise," Oma said. "And that's all."
After Alice finished her snack, she played tag with Bobo
until supper.

The next morning Oma made scrambled eggs for breakfast. She put half the eggs on a plate for Alice. She dished the other half into Bobo's bowl.

Alice grinned at Oma.

"I'm just using up leftovers," Oma said. "And that's all."

After breakfast, Alice practiced with Bobo in the yard.
Oma called to Alice when they were done.

"So?" she said. "How did he do?"

"He sits great!" Alice said. "And he stays great, too!"

"And fetching?" Oma asked.

Alice sighed. "Not so great."

When Alice had left for school, Oma watched Bobo sniffing
the flowers in the yard.

"Eggs for breakfast, proper exercise, and still you won't fetch,
Bobo? What now?"

Oma looked at her old red potholder hanging on the wall.
She looked out at Bobo. She took the potholder off its hook and opened
the door to the backyard.

The night of the dog show, Alice was so nervous at supper
she couldn't eat.

"I'm not so hungry tonight myself," Oma said.

When it was time to leave for Mr. Benjamin's, Alice couldn't find Oma.

"She probably went out for a walk," her mother said. "I'll leave
her a note."

But when they turned on the garage light, there was Oma
sitting in the car.

"I thought I'd come for the ride," she said.

Alice whispered last-minute instructions to Bobo all the way to
Mr. Benjamin's.

At the School for Puppies, Alice and Bobo joined their class.
Oma and Alice's mother found seats in the third row.

"Let's get started," Mr. Benjamin said.

One by one, the schnauzer, the doberman, and the poodle puppies
stayed, sat, and fetched. They each received a blue ribbon.

Then Mr. Benjamin called,
"Alice and Bobo!"
Alice and Bobo walked to the
center of the room.
"Stay, Bobo!" Alice
commanded.
Bobo stayed.

"Sit, Bobo!"
Bobo sat down.
"He might pass after all,"
Alice's mother whispered to Oma.

Mr. Benjamin handed Alice a rubber bone. Alice tossed it high in the air.

"Fetch, Bobo!"

Bobo stayed.

"Fetch!"

Bobo scratched his side.

"I'm sorry, Alice," Mr. Benjamin began, but he was interrupted by a commotion in the third row…

Oma was on her feet! She was waving an old red potholder
above her head.

"*Achtung,* Bobo!" she cried. She tossed the potholder across the room.
"Fetch! *Herbringen!*"

Bobo's ears perked up. His tail thumped the floor.

Then he stood up!

Bobo trotted over to the potholder, and, triumphantly, he carried it back to Oma in the third row.

"Hurray!" Alice cheered. "We passed. I knew we would. Hurray!"

On the way home, in the back seat, Alice sat by the right window. She stroked Bobo's blue ribbon.

Oma sat on the left. Her red potholder lay neatly in her lap.

And Bobo, wagging his tail, lay happily in between.